CLICK, CLACK,
GOOD NIGHT

written by Doreen Cronin   illustrated by Betsy Lewin

A Caitlyn Dlouhy Book · Atheneum Books for Young Readers · New York · London · Toronto · Sydney · New Delhi

A ATHENEUM BOOKS FOR YOUNG READERS • An imprint of Simon & Schuster Children's Publishing Division

1230 Avenue of the Americas, New York, New York 10020

Text copyright © 2020 by Doreen Cronin

All rights reserved, including the right of reproduction in whole or in part in any form.

Illustrations copyright © 2020 by Betsy Lewin

ATHENEUM BOOKS FOR YOUNG READERS is a registered trademark of Simon & Schuster, Inc.

Atheneum logo is a trademark of Simon & Schuster, Inc.

For information about special discounts for bulk purchases, please contact Simon & Schuster
Special Sales at 1-866-506-1949 or business@simonandschuster.com.

The Simon & Schuster Speakers Bureau can bring authors to your live event. For more information or to
book an event, contact the Simon & Schuster Speakers Bureau at 1-866-248-3049 or visit our website at
www.simonspeakers.com.

Book design by Dan Potash.

The illustrations for this book were rendered in watercolor.

The text for this book was set in Filosofia.

Manufactured in China   0720 SCP   First Edition   10 9 8 7 6 5 4 3 2 1

ISBN 978-1-5344-5108-7

ISBN 978-1-5344-5109-4 (eBook)

CIP data for this book is available from the Library of Congress.

For Ellie

—D. C.

For Briar,

have a great childhood

—B. L.

It is nighttime on the farm.
Everyone is tired.
It is time to relax,
unwind, and unplug.

The cows are ready for bed.
Farmer Brown pats their heads
and turns out the cow light.

Cows in the dark, sound asleep.

The sheep are ready for bed.
Farmer Brown brushes out their tangles
and turns out the sheep light.

Sheep in the dark, sound asleep.

The chickens are ready for bed.
Farmer Brown covers them with a blanket
and turns on the chicken light.

Chickens in the nearly dark, sound asleep.

Duck is not quite ready for bed.

Farmer Brown sings him a song,

reads him a book,

turns on the white-noise machine, and
puts on a shadow puppet show,

but Duck is wide-awake.

Farmer Brown practices
downward-facing dog with him,

discusses the day's top news stories,

debates the day's top news stories,

and turns out the duck light.

Farmer Brown in the dark, sound asleep.

Duck in the dark, wide-awake.

Duck tries to sleep like a cow.
But it is too crowded.

Duck tries to sleep like a sheep.
But it is too soft.

Duck tries to sleep like a chicken.
But it is too bright.

Duck finds a soft spot under the maple tree.

No cows.
No sheep.
No chickens.
It's not too soft.
It's not too crowded.

The moonlight is just right.

Duck closes his eyes.

Chit, chat, chitter.

Chit, chat, chitter.

Chit, chat, chitter.

The bats in the trees are wide-awake.

Duck finds a spot by the pond.
No cows.
No sheep.
No chickens.
No bats.

It is not too soft.
It is not too crowded.
There is no chit, chat, chittering.
The moonlight is just right.

Duck closes his eyes.

Burp, burp, ba-burp.

Burp, burp, ba-burp.

Burp, burp, ba-burp.

The frogs in the pond are wide-awake.

Duck knows a new spot.
No cows.
No sheep.
No chickens.
No bats.
No frogs.

Duck also knows where Farmer Brown keeps
the hot sauce, the sliced cheese,
and the whole wheat bread.

His stomach is full.
The mattress is firm.
The book is just right.
Farmer Brown's pajamas are soft.

The moonlight shines in through
the window.

Duck closes his eyes.

Duck in the dark, sound asleep.